When We Go Walking

by CARI BEST   illustrated by KYRSTEN BROOKER

Amazon Children's Publishing

For Gypsy and Jennie, Geri and Annie, Ellen and Gobi,
and especially for Grandma, who always said, "I have to walk!"—C.B.

For John, Nicholas, and Kieran—my walking buddies—K.B.

All rights reserved. Amazon Publishing
Attn: Amazon Children's Publishing, P.O. Box 400818, Las Vegas, NV 89140
www.amazon.com/amazonchildrenspublishing

Library of Congress Cataloging-in-Publication available upon request.

9781477816486 (hardcover)
9781477866481 (e-book)

The illustrations are rendered in oil paint and collage on gessoed paper.
Book design by Katrina Damkoehler. Editor: Melanie Kroupa

Printed in China (R)
First edition
10 9 8 7 6 5 4 3 2 1

When we go walking
on Rambling Road . . .

. . . everyone goes!
Even Abby, our cat.
Mama takes her looking glasses.
Papa takes our baby, Abe.
Abby takes her tabby self.
And I take my collecting bag.

What will we find today?

"A sparrow on a nest!" says Mama.
"The morning city train!" says Papa.
"Red!" says our baby, Abe.
And I say, "Look! A lucky number 5 to put in my
collecting bag because that's how old I am!"

"Good thing you're wearing your walking shoes, Wendy," says Mama.
"Good thing you have your collecting bag, Wendy," says Papa.
"Green!" says our baby, Abe.
And I say, "Wow! An old bell from a bicycle
that still rings when I ping it."

When we go walking on Rambling Road,
bikers bike, runners run, scooters scoot,
and finders find:

"A turtle on a rock!" says Mama.
"An airplane in the sky!" says Papa.
"Blue!" says our baby, Abe.

And I say, "A pretty see-through butterfly
with one small piece that's missing."

When we go walking on Rambling Road,
everyone sings. Even Abby, our cat.

"Walk, walk, walk ourselves
Gently down the street.
Merrily, merrily, merrily, merrily,
We have happy feet."

But my feet aren't always happy, because in the spring it rains too much,
and sometimes my socks get soaked. Then I wish I'd find an umbrella.
But wouldn't you know—I don't.

I find something better.
A flag with faded stripes and stars
that wiggles when I wave it!

Numbers and letters, ribbon and string. A bucket, a balloon,
a wheel from a wagon. A pencil that works. A clock that doesn't.
A penny, a picture, a circle, a square.
A broken word in need of glue that Papa says spells "PEACE."

"Do you *really* need all that?" Papa asks.
And I say, "I *really* do!"

How did they get here,
these things I collect?

Did they fall out of
some place like a pocket?

Did the wind blow them here?

Or were they let go
by a busy bird
trying to build his nest?

When we go walking on Rambling Road, snakes snake, ducks duck, lookers look, and sometimes I get so summer sweaty, my shoes don't want to move.

But I make them move to get this shovel that I just have to have.
Then I muscle my legs like Wonder Girl's and lug it up the hill.

"Do you *really* need that?"
Mama asks.
And I say, "I *really* do."

Some things belong here.
Like rocks and trees and animals.
And every kind of bug.

And some things don't.

Like donut bags and soda cans and greasy pizza boxes.

We put those in a giant sack and leave them at the DUMP.

DUMP: a word I learned on Rambling Road, like

 and  and

When we go walking on Rambling Road,
Mama says, "A squirrel with acorn cheeks!"
Papa says, "A lot of autumn leaves!"
Baby Abe says, "Yellow!"
And I say, "A beach ball! It's a mini world."
Even Mama and Papa like that one.

At home I look at all my treasures. I remember where I found each one.
Oodles and oodles and oodles of things. I can't wait to find some more.
But . . .

One day when we go walking, everyone needs a hat.

Mama says, "It looks like snow!"

Papa says, "It smells like snow!"

Baby Abe says, "White!"

And I say, "Quick! Before my toes freeze frozen,

I need this one last thing."

Then . . .

I shut myself up in my toasty room. Just me and my collection.
While Rambling Road gets buried in winter,
and no one can walk for days.
But *I* can walk inside my room, thinking as I go.
Now's the time to really decide.

What do I want to do?

Sometimes a girl
needs time.

And cookies,
and milk,

and pears,
and apples . . .

. . . until everything comes together.
Now I can invite my family in to see what I've been doing.

"A turkey!" says Mama.
"A robot!" says Papa.
"Purple!" says our baby, Abe,
while Abby the tabby says, "Hissss!"
"It's Rambling Road!" I tell them all
and hold my sign up high.

RAMBLING ROAD

"Bravo, Wendy, Wonder Girl!"
Everyone oohs and aahs.
I feel like a magician after a magic show
and thank everyone for coming.

Then we drink hot chocolate
and taste two cakes.
But my feet are itching to go.
So . . .

I grab a shovel—I know just where to find one—
to get us on our way . . .

...back to walking on Rambling Road.
What will we find today?